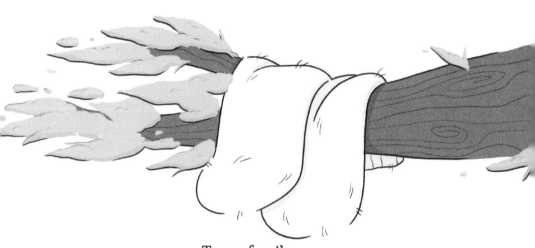

To my family,
Thanks for helping let my dreams fly.
- Isabelle

A Note to Parents & Caregivers—

Reading Stars books are designed to build confidence in the earliest of readers. Relying on word repetition and visual cues, each book features fewer than 50 words.

You can help your child develop a lifetime love of reading right from the very start. Here are some ways to help your beginning reader get going:

 Read the book aloud as a first introduction

 Run your fingers below the words as you read each line

 Give your child the chance to finish the sentences or read repeating words while you read the rest.

 Encourage your child to read aloud every day!

Every Child can be a Reading Star!

Published in the United States by
Xist Publishing
www.xistpublishing.com

First Edition
eISBN: 978-1-5324-1571-5
Paperback ISBN: 978-1-5324-1572-2
Hardcover ISBN: 978-1-5324-1573-9

Download a free eBook copy of this book using this QR code.*

or at https://xist.pub/e8bf8

* Limited time only
Your name and a valid email address are required to download.
Must be redeemed by persons over 13

Fox
Needs Socks

Juliana O'Neill

Isabelle Pichay

xist Publishing

Fox needs
new socks.

Not small socks.

Not big socks.

Not socks
with holes.

Not smelly socks.

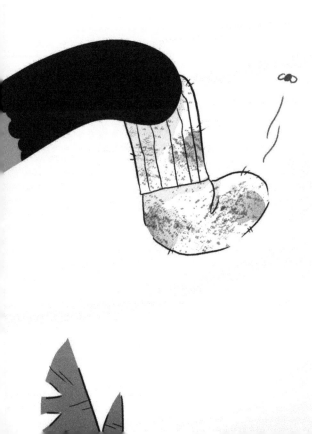

Not socks that
do not match.

13

Fox needs good socks.

Why does fox need socks?

Fox needs socks for a sock hop.

20

Fox needs
hopping socks.

21

I am a Reading Star
because I can read the
words in this book:

a	need
big	needs
do	new
does	not
for	small
fox	smelly
good	sock
holes	socks
hop	that
hopping	why
match	with

xist Publishing